FLL

THE NIGHT RAID

To the staff and pupils of Summer Fields Oxford,
with thanks for your inspiration and input!

First published in 2014 in Great Britain by
Barrington Stoke Ltd
18 Walker Street, Edinburgh, EH3 7LP

www.barringtonstoke.co.uk

Text © 2014 Caroline Lawrence

A CIP catalogue record for this book is available
from the British Library upon request

ISBN: 978-1-78112-366-9

Printed in China by Leo

THE NIGHT RAID

CAROLINE LAWRENCE

This story is taken from the ninth book of Virgil's Aeneid, *an epic poem about the wanderings and battles of the hero Aeneas after the fall of Troy. It was written in Latin shortly before the birth of Christ.*

— EURYALUS —

I was young when they killed me. Just a teenager.

They say death on the battlefield wins you true glory.

They say when someone stabs you it doesn't hurt.

They say it feels like a fist has punched you. That you hardly notice it, in the heat of the battle.

They are wrong.

You DO notice when someone plunges a sword into your body.

It doesn't feel like a fist has punched you. It feels like a heavy, iron, double-edged sword has stabbed you. The blade pierces your skin, parts your muscles, scrapes your bones and pops your organs.

It burns cold. Freezes hot. Then it makes you want to puke.

It does not feel glorious.

It hurts like Hades.

Which is where I am bound.

1

DESTRUCTION

I was ten the first time I saw Rye.

It was on the worst night of my life.

I was on the run.

Rye was a small dark shape at the side of the road. Across the street a house was on fire. I had slowed to a jog because the road went downhill there. Pools of blood made the paving stones slippery.

Rye was crouched beside the body of a man in the gutter.

A clatter of tiles came from the other side of the street as the roof of the burning house collapsed. Flames burst out between the stone pillars of the porch. The bright yellow light showed me the scene. A boy of about five or six, with black curls and pale skin. He was trying to take the sword from the dead man's hand.

I was running for my life. So I passed him by. I had seen enough death in one hour to last a lifetime. What did one more matter?

But then the moon came out from behind a cloud and I heard the goddess whisper in my head. "Help him," she said.

I stopped, closed my eyes and prayed to her. "If you want me to help him then you must help me, Diana."

When I turned to look back, I saw the whole town on fire. Black buildings within orange flames. Sparks flying. And I could hear the screams of men, women and children.

Every part of my body wanted to run, but I made myself go back towards the little boy. I crouched down on the other side of the body.

I pretended to be calm. "Hello," I said. "I'm Nisus. What's your name?"

"Euryalus," he said. "But they call me Rye." He was still trying to pull the fingers off the handle of the sword. But the man's death grip would not let it go.

I looked at the dead man. He had straight eyebrows and curly black hair. I looked at the boy. He had curly black hair, too. And straight black eyebrows, drawn together in a scowl. His bottom lip stuck out. At first I thought his face was smudged with mulberry jam. Then I saw it was blood.

"Is this your father?" I said.

He nodded. "They killed him. So I am going to kill them. He showed me how."

"You can't kill them, Rye," I said.

"He showed me how," the little boy repeated. "He told me I had to protect Mama."

The smoke made my eyes blink. How could his father have said such a thing?

"You can't kill them," I said. "They're big and you are small."

For the first time he lifted his gaze and looked at me. His eyes brimmed with tears. They also blazed with black anger.

"Rye," I said, "there are too many of them. And they will be here any minute."

"They killed Papa." He stood up, planted his feet apart, clenched his fists. "I hate them!" he spat.

"I know," I said. "I hate them, too. And one day we will take revenge. But now is not that time." I stood up and held out my hand. "Come with me," I said. "I promise I'll teach you how to fight. And one day we will kill them."

He looked up at me, his eyes wet and blazing at the same time.

"Promise?" he said.

"I promise. I swear on the moon goddess Diana, my family's protector." I pointed up. "See? She has come out from behind that little cloud. She will guide us to safety. Hurry!"

He shook his head, his lower lip still pushed out. "I have to stay and protect Mama."

I stared at him. "Your mother is still alive?"

He nodded.

"Where?" I asked.

He took my hand and tugged. His little fingers were slick with his father's blood.

Rye pulled me between two slender marble pillars into an open doorway. I found myself in a courtyard open to the sky. Moonlight sucked the colour from the world. Everything was black, grey or silver. In the smoky darkness between pillars of a walkway, I saw a big square loom for weaving cloth.

"There she is." Rye pointed to the loom. I saw a pair of silk slippers in the gap between the bottom of the cloth and the floor.

"You must come now," I warned her. "The warriors are coming."

The slippers did not move and no sound came from behind the loom.

A whisper of dread prickled my backbone.

I stepped forward and pushed the loom aside. A woman crouched in the shadow of a pillar.

"No!" she cried. She put up her arms to protect her head. "Don't hurt me!"

"I'm not going to hurt you," I said. "I'm here to help you."

"Where's Rye?" she whimpered. "What have you done to my little boy?"

"He's right here," I said. "He's safe. We must go. Before they come back."

"No!" She shook her head. "My husband. He told me to hide."

"Your husband is dead," I said. "He can't help you. But I can. Come with me. With Diana's help I'll protect you. You and your little boy."

The moon went behind a small cloud, as if she had slipped behind a curtain.

"No!" Rye's mother sobbed. She shook her head. "You're only a boy yourself. How can you help us?"

Fear gave my mouth a sour taste, but I lifted my face to the moon goddess. "Diana," I prayed. "Please give us a sign."

I hoped the goddess would appear from the cloud to give my words power. But she did something much better. She fired a flaming arrow. We all saw it streak up into the star-spattered dome of the sky.

"Look, Mama!" Rye pointed. "A shooting star!"

At last his mother came out of the shadows. She looked up. We all watched the orange light rise up to the top of the night sky, then sink down to the east. Towards Mount Ida.

It left a trail of fire that glowed.

"Like a rainbow in the night," Rye said. He wiped his cheek. It left a dark streak of blood on his sleeve.

"It's more than a star," his mother whispered. "It's a sign."

I nodded.

She clutched my hand. I could feel the hard patches of skin the weaving had left on her fingers. Just like my mother's hands. My dead mother's hands. I pushed the thought aside. No time for grief now.

"Come," I said. "We'll go the way Diana's arrow pointed. Towards Ida."

Rye's mother nodded and squeezed my hand. "The moon goddess must like you," she said. Then she held out her free hand to the boy. "Come, baby. Let's go with ..."

She looked at me.

"Nisus," I said. "My name is Nisus."

"I'm not a baby!" Rye cried. "And I want to hold Nisus's hand."

I almost smiled. "I have two hands," I said. "One for each of you."

So I held his hand in my right and hers in my left and I led them out of the dim courtyard towards the flame-lit street.

As we passed out of the double doors, Rye's mother let go of my hand and threw her arms around one of the pillars. She kissed it and pressed her cheek to the cool marble. "Oh, my dear house," she cried. "How I loved you."

She did not see the body of her husband lying in the gutter. I was glad of it. I took her hand again and pulled her towards the road. Towards the Ida Gate.

Behind us I could hear the shouts of men. They were coming – the Greeks who had butchered my family and burned my city.

Hand in hand in hand, the three of us hurried down the bloody street. Two children and a woman. Running for our lives from the burning city – Troy.

2

THE GROVE

I don't remember much else about that night. Only flashes.

I remember that the black arch of the town gate smelled like a giant's mouth.

I remember that families hid among the tombs outside the town wall.

I remember there was an old man riding on a lion that stood on two legs. The lion held a little boy's hand.

When I looked closer, I understood. There was no lion. It was one of our greatest warriors. He was wearing a lion skin, holding his son's hand and carrying his crippled father on his back. The old man was carrying something, too. A jumble of little wooden figures. Their household gods.

I felt a stab of fear. I hadn't taken *our* household gods. Nor had Rye's mother. Which god would protect us?

Then I remembered the goddess of the moon. I looked up. "Diana," I prayed, "please protect us."

Rye was looking at the man in the lion skin. He tugged my tunic. I bent down.

"Is it Hercules?" Rye whispered.

Hercules was a great Greek soldier.

I shook my head. "No. He is one of *our* warriors. Our greatest warrior. His name is Aeneas. He will be our Leader. He will tell us what to do."

And he did.

The man in the lion skin led us up Mount Ida, through a dark forest to a sacred grove of blue-smelling pines. Those trees whispered to us and sang us to sleep that night, but the next morning they squealed and groaned when men started to chop them down.

"Do not be alarmed," our new Leader said in a big voice. "The goddess has given me her blessing to cut down this sacred grove and make ships from the wood. Those trees will protect us on the water as they protected us last night."

People murmured to one another.

"Where are we going?" a child's clear voice cried. It was Rye, asking what nobody else dared to ask.

Our Leader turned to look at him.

"We are going to found a New Troy," he said. "It is our destiny."

3

– SEVEN YEARS –

We sailed to many places and many islands before we found our promised land. In all that time I did not forget my promise to Rye. I taught him how to use an axe, a sword, a javelin and a bow.

We swam and ran, wrestled and boxed. When our Leader's father died, we held funeral games for him. Rye won his first foot race.

The other runners were twice his age.

Our Leader suffered much in the search for a new land, but Rye and I were content. In all those years of wandering, we lived in our own world – training, hunting, running, eating, laughing.

We knew each other so well that we could talk without words – just a pointed finger or a raised eyebrow.

Rye was closer than a brother, dearer than a friend, more loyal than a hound.

4

THE PROMISED LAND

We arrived at our new home on my 17th birthday.

We saw a hundred trees, with flat tops like ladies' parasols. We heard the throb of insects. The land shimmered green and gold between the dark blue sea and the apple sky of dusk.

Our ship was right behind our Leader's. Rye and I stood at the front as she cut through the blue water with her bronze beak. She was like a moving creature beneath us. Her polished planks were as warm and smooth as a girl's cheek.

Our Leader stood at the back of the ship. He turned and gave us a rare smile. Then he pointed towards a thousand birds flying over the flat-topped pines. The birds turned and wheeled together, like a shoal of fish.

"A good omen!" our Leader cried. And it seemed he was speaking to us.

"If he's right and this is our new home," I said to Rye, "we can build a little house near the river. Your mother will weave and we will hunt."

Rye nodded and smiled. "And in the evenings she will cook what we bring home," he said. "We will eat and laugh together."

But there was no hunting that first evening. We had heard that fierce warriors lived nearby. Fear kept us close to the ships. Our Leader said we could explore in the bright light of morning.

Because we were almost out of food, we had to search the ships for something to eat.

In the end we found some old salted venison, and a bag of dried berries. Nowhere near enough for two hundred people. Then someone found a barrel of bread, enough for each person. The flat round loaves were as tough as leather so we used them as plates. But a few mouthfuls of stringy meat and sour berries did not fill our bellies, so some of us started to gnaw the month-old bread.

Our Leader's 12-year-old son Ascanius laughed. "It's like eating a table!" he said.

Our Leader jumped up. "A prophecy told of this!" he cried. "It went, 'When you grind your tables that means you have arrived.' Now here we are using stale bread as tables and grinding them with our teeth!"

"By Hercules!" a man cried. He reached into his mouth and pulled out something that looked like a bloody piece of pottery. "I've broken my tooth on your prophecy!"

Everyone laughed. Our Leader offered up a vow of thanks to his mother Venus, and also to Jupiter. Then he brought out our last cow and made a sacrifice of her there and then. We roasted chunks of meat on pine-twigs and somehow there was enough for everyone.

Rye's mother joined Rye and me at our fire. She looked around and nodded.

"I could live here," she said.

Rye and I smiled at her and at one another. We ate our fill under the purple sky, in the place where we hoped to rebuild Troy.

But the goddess Juno was not finished tormenting us.

5

ALLIES AND ENEMIES

We were at the mouth of a great river called Tiber in a country called Italy.

The good news was that one of the local kings had a daughter. This princess was young, beautiful and rich. Her priests had made a prophecy that she must marry a warrior from abroad. So our Leader sent his best speakers to plead his case. They returned on the backs of fine horses. Her father had agreed! Our Leader and the princess would marry, and we would be allowed to build a New Troy and live in peace.

Then we heard rumours of a warrior named Turnus. He was as fierce as a lion, they said. He had set his heart on marrying the princess. He would fight to the death for her. We all knew who was behind this. Juno. Queen of the Gods. Enemy of Troy.

And so we built a fort. With towers. And a ditch around it.

Some of the men called the fort New Troy. But it was wood, not stone. It was weak, not strong. The ditch was only a ditch, not a moat.

More rumours reached us. They said Turnus had gathered two thousand men. Three thousand. Ten thousand!

So our Leader prepared two ships.

"I am going up the river," he said. "To see a king who hates Turnus. He rules a city of seven hills with a great temple on the highest of them. I will ask this king to be our friend. I will ask him to send some men back with me to help us defend our fort."

The Leader stepped into his ship. "Keep a sharp lookout while I am gone," he said. "If Turnus should come, do not fight him. Stay in the fort. Wait until I return with more men." He turned to his son. "Prince Ascanius," he said. "You are in command."

"Why do we have to stay in the fort?" Rye grumbled after our Leader left.

"We only have to stay there if Turnus comes," I told him.

"But I am ready to fight," said Rye. "I want to fight!"

"You're only 13," I said. And I ruffled his hair.

Rye batted my hand away. "The prince is only 12," he complained. "But he has been put in command of us all."

"Be patient," I said. "Our time will come."

Grey storm clouds boiled up that evening. And the strangest rainbow I have ever seen. It was red, pink and purple against the clouds, and it reminded me of Diana's arrow on that terrible night. The night Troy burned.

Rye pointed at the rainbow. "Look!" he said. "Do you think Juno sent that as a sign to Turnus? To tell him where we are?"

"I hope not," I said.

"I hope *so*!" Rye growled. "I am ready to avenge my father's death." He was butchering a deer we had killed. His arms were red to the elbows.

As it happened, his chance would come sooner than either of us dreamed.

6

ANOTHER SIEGE

The next morning, Rye and I went hunting. Fresh game was always welcome, and we loved to stalk together. In the deep woods beside the river we spotted the tracks of a stag. Without a sound, we followed the track north past pine and laurel. At last we saw him. A fine stag. He stood in a clearing, still as a statue, and turned to look at us. Both our arrows struck him and he fell.

When we went to him, we saw distant buildings through a break in the trees. It was a city built on a curve of the river. We saw seven hills with a temple on the highest of them. It seemed only a few hours' walk to the north, but it was getting late, so we slung the deer on a pole and carried it back to camp.

At home we skinned the deer and butchered it and cooked it over a fire on cool green grass in the shade of a pine tree. Rye took the best part into the fort. He came out again, crossed the ditch we had dug, and sat down beside me. Some of the other off-duty men had joined us.

"Where have you been, Girly Locks?" one of the men asked Rye.

"I took the best part of the roast deer to my mother," Rye said. "They built her a room in the fort."

Another man snorted. "All the other women stayed in Sicily until it was safe to come. But your mother came along with the men."

"Because she is fearless," I said. "Like her son."

The men exchanged glances but didn't say any more.

I looked at Rye. In seven years he had grown into a beautiful young man. The most beautiful of all the Trojans. One of the youngest, too. He had not even started to shave.

We had just finished our food when a warning cry brought us to our feet. We saw a dark cloud rising to the east. Was it a storm? Or something worse?

Rye's vision was sharper than mine. "It's men," he said, and he gripped my arm. "Men on horseback." He laughed. "They are warriors. I can see plumes on some of their helmets."

"Get your weapons!" the lookout screamed from his tower in the fort. "Get inside! Man the ramparts!"

I grabbed my bow and arrows. Rye took our hunting javelins. We sprinted inside, closed the wooden gates, and climbed the stairs to the high walkways behind the spiked walls.

Up on these ramparts we could see at least a thousand horses carrying a thousand armed warriors. They flowed towards us like a huge river. The horses kicked up a great cloud of dust – blood red in the setting sun.

"Down there!" someone cried. "By the gates!"

We looked down.

A small number of mounted soldiers had appeared below us, right outside our gate. These few men had raced ahead of their army. The biggest warrior rode a strange-looking horse. It was white, with splashes of black.

"What's he riding?" someone asked.

"It's a Thracian piebald!" another voice called. "Fast as the wind, fierce as a lion."

"Look at his helmet," Rye breathed. "Gold with a scarlet crest. He must be their commander."

"Turnus," I said.

As if the big man had heard me, he pulled back his arm and threw something. I jumped away as a spear struck the outside of the wall just beneath me. A little higher and the spear would have hit me. My knees started to shake.

"What are you?" the big man yelled. "Men or lambs?" He showed us his bright fangs, like a snarling wolf. "Come down!" he shouted. "Come out and fight, you cowards!"

Rye turned. I held him back. "Remember what our Leader said? We must not fight."

The other men muttered curses as Turnus taunted us. He rode all around the fort, rattling every door and calling up insults.

At last he was below us again. He looked up.

I saw gleaming black eyes behind the slits of his helmet. It made him look part animal and part god.

Then he was looking straight at me.

Our eyes locked. And in that moment, the world shifted.

I am back in Troy as it burns. Out of sight on the roof of our house, I see the warriors pour into our courtyard. I see them stab my father and my brothers. I see them drag away my mother. I hear her screams.

One of the warriors must have seen movement up on the roof, for he lifts his head and looks straight at me. He is terrifying in his bloody helmet. Not human. A killing machine.

That is when I flee. I scramble off the roof tiles. I land hard on the stone pavement at the back of our house. I run in blind terror through the dark backstreets of Troy.

A coward.

I deserted my family in their hour of need.

That is the crime I can never forget.

Now I try to bring myself to the present.
I reach back, grope for an arrow, find it, notch it.
I aim at the warrior in his terrifying helmet with
its nodding crest. I draw my bow and let fly. But
I am no longer strong, 17-year-old Nisus. I am
ten again, with feeble trembling arms. My arrow
does not even touch him. The shame!

My face grows hot, my throat dry. I am glad
it is dusk and that the light is failing.

"You pretty-boy Trojans in your long-sleeved
tunics and leggings!" Turnus shouts up at me.
"Why don't you come down and fight?"

Something like a red curtain falls over my
eyes. There is a buzzing in my ears, as if some
insect has flown into my brain. I draw my sword
and turn towards the stairs that lead down to the
gate.

"Nisus! No!" This time it is Rye who catches
my arm. "Our Leader told us not to fight!"

His voice is far away and muffled by the buzz
in my head. It is easy to shake him off. But other
hands catch me and hold me. "You can't!" they
cry. "Our Leader told us to wait."

"Look!" a man screams. "What are they doing?"

My ears click. My eyes clear. I am myself again.

I look over the parapet. Turnus is riding his piebald horse towards the campfire where we cooked the deer.

"Fire," Turnus roars to his men. "Get fire!"

Now I know what they are going to do.

They are going to set the fort on fire and when we run outside they will butcher us. For every one of us, they have ten men.

It will be like Troy all over again. Only this time none of us will get out alive.

7

NYMPH BOY

Our enemy Turnus spurs his horse towards the fire Rye and I left burning. As he rides past, he bends down and plucks a branch from the glowing coals. Then he pulls himself upright in the saddle. He wheels and holds the sparkling stick up high. His twenty companions follow his lead.

I see fat smoke flow back from the swooping torches. I smell the burning pine pitch. I hear his war cry, like the red-raw howl of a wolf.

"They're going to set fire to our fort!" Rye gasps. "They'll burn us alive!" He looks at me with wide eyes. "My mother!" he cries. "I've got to get her out of here!"

Rye turns to go down from the high walkway.

"Wait!" I say. "Look!"

We watch Turnus ride towards a low hill by the river. The hill is black against the purple sky.

Rye grips my arm. "He wants to fight as much as I do! He's trying to lure us out of the fort ..."

"By threatening to burn our ships!" I gasp. My stomach sinks like a pebble in a bucket.

I remember how the sacred trees cried and moaned when we cut them down, but let us carve them into ships. They kept us safe for seven years and brought us to our new land. I remember the feel of the wood, as smooth and warm as a girl's skin under my hand.

The thought of our faithful boats being devoured by flames breaks my heart.

"No!" I cry.

But Turnus and his riders have disappeared behind the hill.

There is a moment of stillness. Then we all see the orange flare of a sail. It is like a butterfly on fire, bright against the violet dusk.

Then another burns. And another. Sparks fly up. Smoke, too.

"No!" I cry again.

As if in answer to my cry, the smoke is snuffed out. Then I see something I cannot believe. There are pale forms in the dark water. Like dolphins! Or girls swimming! They swim towards the river mouth. Towards the sea.

I peer into the gathering darkness. "What are those creatures in the water?" I say.

"What?" asks Rye.

"Like dolphins," I whisper. "Or naked girls." I feel my cheeks grow hot. But I know what I have seen!

Someone laughs. "Naked girls? What are you on about?"

He tells the others, and they laugh, too.

"Wait!" Rye cries. "I see them."

Then a spear of lightning slashes the sky and the men are silenced by the longest, deepest clap of thunder I have ever heard. A great roar from Jupiter.

In the thunder, I seem to hear the words, "Go free, goddesses of the ocean. Go free!"

And suddenly I know what I have seen.

"They're nymphs!" I shout. "The ships were made from sacred wood from Ida's Grove. Jupiter has turned them into nymphs to save them!"

"Nymphs?" The men around me start to laugh. For a moment their fear is forgotten. They gave Rye the nickname 'Girly Locks' a year ago. Now they give me one, too – 'Nymph Boy'.

I know their jokes are friendly, but it stings my pride.

"He's right!" the lookout cries from his wooden tower. "The ships have gone. But I can see ... By the gods!"

A hush falls over the fort. The little hairs on my arms lift up.

We can all see the nymphs now. There are at least a dozen of them. Swimming through the black and glassy water.

In the holy silence we hear Turnus bellow to his men.

"Don't be afraid!" he shouts. "This was not a sign against us! It was a sign against them!" He points his spear at us. "Now they can't escape!"

he gloats. "Without their ships, the sea becomes a watery prison. And the land is ours, so where can they go? They say they have a destiny? Well, I have a destiny, too. To kill them and reclaim my bride!"

He rides towards us, still pointing his spear. "You cowards!" he screams. "You think a wooden fence can protect you when the stone walls of Troy could not? We won't come by night in the belly of a wooden horse like those Greek cowards. We will come tomorrow in the full light of day. Then we will destroy you once and for all."

Our men look at one another.

"You should have died seven years ago when they burned Troy," Turnus cries. "But tomorrow you will at last meet the fate you deserve! I will do what the Greeks could not! I will send you all to Hades!"

8

NIGHT FALLS

It is dark now, but we can see the shapes of two thousand men encamped around us, just the other side of the ditch. They are so close that we can hear them. Their laughter. Their drunken songs. Even the rattle of dice.

"Come, Rye," I say, and I turn away from the view of enemy fires. "We're on guard duty in two hours. Let's get a cupful of sleep."

He nods. We go down in silence and stretch out by one of the fires. But I can't sleep. The sounds of saw and hammer fill the night. Men are building walkways from one tower to another, so they can reach different parts of the fort when the attack comes.

I stare up into the dome of night.

The stars do not meet my gaze but look away. Distant. Cool. Aloof.

Beside me, Rye whimpers in his sleep.

Then he cries out.

"Rye," I whisper. "Don't be afraid. It's only a dream."

Rye's eyes are open. Haunted. He pushes himself up and sits facing me with his legs crossed. One side of him is lit red by the dying fire. His other side is in darkness. He turns his head to stare at the low flames.

"Nisus," he says. "What happens when we die?"

I sit up, too, and cross my own legs. Our knees almost touch. "You know what happens," I say. "Our Leader told us about it."

Our Leader had been to Hades and returned. A thing no man had done before.

Rye nods. "There are levels, aren't there?" he says. "A sunny place for the brave. A dark swamp for those who take their own lives."

"Yes," I whisper. Then I add, "I hope I go to the sunny place."

He nods. "Me, too." Then he turns his head to look at me. "But I don't care where I go after death, as long as we're together."

I swallow hard. I can't trust my voice, so I just nod.

Rye grips my hands. His fingers are very cold.

"Flame Head," he whispers. "Turnus is like Flame Head."

Flame Head is the name we Trojans gave the fiercest Greek of all. When we were young, his real name was too long and too horrible to say out loud. It still is.

"Flame Head?" I frown. "You saw Flame Head?"

Rye nods. "He killed my father."

I stare at him. "But you were only six. How can you remember?"

"How can I forget?" Rye shudders. "He had the same helmet, with slits like almonds. I saw his eyes looking out at me."

I shudder, too, and pull the blanket around me. "But Flame Head had red hair," I point out. "Turnus is dark. You can tell from his beard."

"I know," Rye whispers. "But Turnus has the same eyes and teeth as Flame Head. And the same laugh."

"Laugh?" I say. "When did you ever hear Flame Head laugh?"

Rye bites his lip. "When he had my father in a neck lock. He saw me with my dagger and said, 'Come on little warrior, save him if you can.'"

I feel sick.

Rye goes on. "He took the dagger from my limp fingers and used it to kill my father. Then he laughed."

"He killed your father before your eyes?" I gasp.

Rye nods.

"Then what?" I ask.

"He put my dagger in his belt and ran off to butcher more people."

I try to swallow, but my throat is too dry.

"That's why I'm going to kill Turnus," Rye says. And the old look is back in his eyes. The black fire of anger.

"No, Rye," I say. "You can't."

"Yes, I can," he insists. "I'm ready. You've taught me well."

"You've only killed animals until now," I say. "Killing a person is different."

"I'm going to kill him," he repeats. "It's what I've waited all my life to do."

"It was Flame Head who killed your father," I remind him. "Not Turnus."

"If I can kill Turnus," Rye says, "it will feel almost as good as killing Flame Head."

He takes a breath, like a swimmer before he dives. "It was my fault my father died," he says. "He showed me how to use a dagger. I had it in my hand but I couldn't protect him."

"You were only six!" I say.

"I know that," he tells me, "in my head. But my heart feels shame."

We are still sitting with our legs crossed. Facing one another. Blankets over us like cloaks.

Rye's head is down. His hands are still in mine. His fingers are warmer now. But they tremble. Or is it my fingers that shake?

"I, too, feel shame," I say. Then I confess what I have never told anyone else until now.

"I saw men in helmets, too," I tell him. "I ran away while they killed my family."

"But you were only ten!" he says.

We look up and give the same sad smile. We understand each other perfectly. We both know we were too young to fight. But somehow it does not take away the burn of shame.

Rye clenches his fists and bares his teeth. "If only our Leader hadn't made us promise not to fight," he says. "I'm ready now."

"What can we do?" I say. "There are nearly two thousand of them and only two hundred of us. We are completely outnumbered."

9

THE PLAN

"What can we do?" Those were my words. But now, as I stand on the parapet and watch the enemy sleep, a thought flashes behind my eyes. Like Diana's burning arrow.

I can see a path that leads north into the woods.

"Rye," I say. "Do you see the woods where we hunted the stag this morning? Remember how we saw a city with seven hills, and a temple on the highest of them?"

Rye nods. "Look! Their watch fires are almost out. I can hear them snoring. Gods! I can smell the wine from here."

Another arrow of an idea sticks in my heart and flares up – a chance to be a hero and gain glory. I feel as if I've swallowed a burning coal. A coal of excitement, joy, terror. My heart beats so hard I think I might faint. I have to hang on to the sharpened points of the fort's wall in case my knees give way.

"Does this desire come from the gods?" I say to myself. "Or from my own heart?"

Rye gives me a sharp look. "What desire?"

I can't meet his gaze. "Two hundred can't fight two thousand," I say. "But what if one man could get through?"

"What do you mean?" he asks.

I turn to look at him. When we stand this close, I have to look down, for he is a head shorter than I am. "The city we saw this morning," I say. "On a curve of the river. Our Leader must be there! If I can get to him and bring help, think of the glory I would gain us." My next words come fast. "If they offer a reward," I say, "I would give it to you! For me, the honour is enough."

I expect him to look up at me with pride but instead his dark eyes fill with angry tears. "You would go without me?" he asks.

I grip his arms. Under the cloth of his tunic his skin is cool.

"Rye, you're not even 14," I say. "You're too young to die."

"You told me you would train me," he protests. "You said we would kill them together."

"I know," I say. "But this way, if I die and you survive, then a part of me would live on. Don't you see?"

He does see. And his eyes are full of pain.

"Besides," I force a laugh, "I need you to give me a proper funeral if I don't make it!"

"How can you joke about it?" Rye snaps.

My smile fades. "What if I take you with me, and you are hurt or killed?" I ask. "What would I tell your mother? Of all the mothers, she was the only one who gave up a safe home in Sicily to be with her son."

Rye blinks. His eyes have lost their blurred look. Now they are sharp and clear.

"I'm coming with you!" he says. "And nothing you say will change my mind."

My stomach sinks at the thought of what could happen to him. But my heart lifts at the thought of gaining glory with him at my side.

"Look!" Rye points. "Here comes the midnight shift. Let's go tell the elders our idea."

And before I can stop him, he's off down the wooden stairs. He takes them two at a time. I greet the two warriors who will take our places. Then I hurry after him.

When I catch up to him, he says, "Two hundred can't fight two thousand. But two can!"

10

THE ELDERS

It is after midnight. The fort has fallen silent as men gulp a few hours of sleep, but the elders are still awake.

They are apart from the rest, in the centre of the camp. An inner fence protects them. When I tell the guard we have a plan, he stands aside to let us pass. As we enter, I see Prince Ascanius and four of the elders. They stand around a campfire and lean on their spears. Half their bodies are lit by yellow firelight, half are in darkness. Half their bodies are hot, half cool.

The Prince looks up, sees us, comes to greet us. "What news?" he asks.

He is only 12, but he has the confidence of a man twice his age.

Rye and I both speak at once, a thing that hardly ever happens.

"Nisus, you speak first," the Prince says, "for you are older."

One of the elders smiles and whispers in the ear of another, "Look. It's Girly Locks and Nymph Boy."

A third one smirks.

"Yes, Trojans, we are young," I say. "Don't be put off by this. For we have a plan. Turnus and his men are drunk and half their fires have gone out. Rye and I often hunt along the river. Today we went north. We think we know a way through to the place our Leader has gone – the city of seven hills."

The elders look at each other in amazement.

"You can get to our Leader?" one says. "And tell him what has happened?"

I nod. "I believe so."

"But he sailed there three days ago," says another elder. "Only he and the men who sailed with him know where the city is. None of us have ever seen it."

"We saw it yesterday," Rye jumps in. "Through a break in trees. By a bend of the river. A city with seven hills and a temple on the highest. That must be it. We can be there and back by dawn."

"With our Leader and his new army!" I add.

The elders look at each other.

Then they turn back to us with shining eyes.

They embrace us, praise us, shake our hands.

The Prince weeps. They all weep.

If we can get to our Leader and bring him back with more troops, then our New Troy is safe.

I didn't expect it to be this easy to convince the elders. They must be desperate.

They *are* desperate!

They promise us vast treasure if we can pull it off. Bowls full of jewels. Chests full of gold. Land and slaves, male and female.

Prince Ascanius promises me the horse and armour of Turnus.

Then he turns to Rye. "When I become King," he says, "you will be my advisor, my right-hand man."

Rye's eyes are bright. Like black coals. "All I ask is that you care for my mother, if anything happens to me," he says. "Give her the land and slaves you promised me, so she won't spend every moment weaving at her loom."

"More than that," Ascanius says. "She will be like the mother I lost on the night they burned Troy."

Once again they embrace us.

The Prince gives Rye his own sword. It is razor-sharp and has an ivory scabbard.

One of the elders gives me his lion skin. He drapes it over me. It is heavy, soft, warm.

"You look like Hercules," Rye whispers as two of the elders take us to the gate. "Or our Leader on the night we left Troy. Do you remember?"

"How can I forget?" I laugh. "We thought he was a lion on two legs!"

"Now *you* are the lion on two legs!" Rye laughs.

The gates of the wooden fort close behind us. We find ourselves in the boggy ditch – the only thing that separates us from two thousand enemy soldiers.

It all happened so fast.

From the walls behind and above, I hear Prince Ascanius whisper something down at us. But the hot blood is too loud in my ears. I cannot catch any of his words.

Something tickles the back of my brain, like a loose thread.

Have I forgotten something?

I can't think. In any case, there is no going back now.

The moment has come.

The moment Rye and I have been training for since Troy fell.

Now is the time for us to prove our courage and win True Glory.

– EURYALUS –

When I was little, I wanted to be Icarus, the boy who flew.

Icarus and his father were trapped on an island by an evil king. But every night, Icarus's father worked on a secret project. An invention made of reeds and feathers and wax.

First he formed the reeds into four frames and tied them with leather thongs.

Then he stuck on beeswax that smelled of honey.

And then ten thousand bird feathers.

He was making wings. Two pairs.

One for the father, one for the son.

Huge wings. Massive. But light and strong.

One summer day the wings were ready.

Father and son carried them up to the highest peak on the island.

And flew.

Now, like Icarus, I can fly.

My wish has come true.

But I have been in flight too long. Now I want to have my feet on earth. To press my bare soles on grass or sand or granite warmed by the sun. To feel the breeze in my hair. To smell pine-sap or sea-water. Or dust on dew. To taste sticky honey, or bitter dandelion root, or sweet roast boar. I can hear and I can see, but they are pale senses without the others.

Sometimes I feel like I want to vomit. But I have nothing to vomit up. And nothing to vomit from.

I have no stomach. I have no mouth. I have no body.

I am a floating thing. I see, but am never seen. I hear, but am never heard.

I hover over strange places.

I am safe, but I miss taste, touch, smell.

Those senses can hurt us, but oh how they give us pleasure.

I would give anything to feel pain in a tooth again. Or hunger. To smell a skunk. Or sweat. I would love to sleep. But I am not tired. I have no appetite. I feel no desire.

Why?

Why am I still here? When can I be released?

Please, gods, help me find the answer.

11

ACROSS THE DITCH

The moon goddess, Diana, has licked the colour from the world. She has left it black and silver.

Rye and I are climbing up out of a soggy ditch. A smell of brackish water prickles my nose. Cold night mud squeezes between my toes. We creep up the slope of the ditch and peep over, ready to run if someone raises the alarm.

In dying firelight, I can see the shapes of men. Some sit with their backs against trees or on folded blankets. But most of them are lying down, their arms and legs flung wide. They snore, uncovered, for it is a mild night. Their horses crop the grass and their chariots are flipped on their ends with their poles standing up.

"Where are the watchmen?" Rye whispers.

"I think these *are* the watchmen," I reply.

Rye makes a strange noise. Is he crying? No. He's giggling.

I stare at him. "What is it?"

The moonlight shows me his teeth in a bright grin. "The men are down and the chariots are up," he whispers. "But it should be the other way around. For their enemy is among them – us!" He bites his lip to keep from laughing.

Then he brings his mouth to my ear.

"I know our mission is to find our Leader and bring him back with more men, but what if we killed just a few? Along the way?"

Gods! He is fearless! But I can't resist it.

"All right," I whisper. "But let me lead. You follow. And watch my back."

12

REVENGE

I rise up out of the ditch. My sword is in my right hand. It feels light, alert, hungry for blood.

This afternoon I sharpened it.

Just as Rye's mother sits at her wooden spinning wheel and makes wool, I sat at a spinning disc of stone and made a razor-sharp edge. The metal sent up sparks. The blade yelped against the stone.

I have killed men from a distance. Shot them with arrows. Thrown spears into a line of them. But I have never attacked a man with a sword. I have never killed up close.

I see a man propped up on folded rugs. His legs are straight out before him, his arms limp. His head droops on his snoring chest.

He is not much older than I am.

I sweep my sword below his chin.

Something topples off his body and rolls at my feet. It is his head – still asleep! As his empty neck spouts purple, I gasp and jump back.

I am sick with excitement.

I move forward, and my sword takes off three more heads. How easy it is! Like slicing mushrooms. I move across the grass, which is now slippery with blood as well as dew.

My heart races. My skin hums. My eyes are open wide.

A boy who is almost as pretty as Rye sleeps on some blankets. There is a faint smile on his face. He puffs out wine fumes and there is a dice box in his loose grip. He won at dice, but he might have been luckier had he stayed awake and gambled a little longer.

Off comes his head. The eyes fly open and gaze at me in horror.

I hear a noise to my left and see that Rye has also scattered half a dozen heads like dice. Those men had been sleeping, but now he is going for a man who is awake. The man is crouching behind one of those big bowls they use to mix wine and water.

As Rye comes close, the man stands up. He is a head taller than my friend.

My heart is in my mouth. What if the man fights back?

But the man's eyes are wide and rolling with terror. He opens his mouth to say something, then looks down at the sword buried in his chest. Rye has plunged it in up to the hilt. His fist is still on the handle.

The man gives a puzzled smile. He cannot understand why a beautiful boy with long curls and white skin would stab him. He opens his mouth to say "Why?"

For an answer, Rye yanks out the sword and moves on. The man slumps to his knees. He vomits up his life spirit along with scarlet blood and purple wine.

I remember the first time I saw Rye. His six-year-old face smeared with blood as he tried to tug the sword from his father's death grip.

Now, at last, his thirst for blood is being quenched.

I shiver with pleasure. I, too, feel the thrill that killing brings.

The two boys who ran from Troy as it burned have proved themselves at last.

We are not cowards.

We are heroes.

No! We are more than heroes. In that moment, we are gods.

13

PLUNDER

One mistake, one slip, one sound could prove fatal. But I am drunk with excitement and power. I feel immortal. There is some kind of juice running through my body.

Rye runs over, his sword dripping. "Nisus, let's take a few prizes to give to our Leader when we see him," he says. "To prove what we did."

I nod. We search the bodies for treasure. I find a gold breastplate. Rye lifts a gold studded belt. But those are too heavy to carry.

Then Rye gasps. He points at the grass. "It's almost as fine as the one Turnus wears!"

It is a glittering bronze helmet, with nodding plumes of scarlet.

Rye holds it up. Admires it. Puts it on.

It transforms him from a beautiful boy into a warrior with almond slits for eyes.

He turns to me and I see his perfect smile under the bronze nose guard.

He looks like an animal. Or a god. But not human.

"Come on!" I whisper. My voice sounds clogged. "We mustn't forget our mission."

"What?" he says, too loud. "I can't hear you!"

I put my finger to my lips. I point towards the woods. It's a sign we use when we hunt in silence. I bend my finger to beckon him. I want him to follow me to the city of seven hills.

Rye nods his inhuman head. The crest nods, too, like a sliding snake.

We hurry to the shelter of the woods. Something tugs at the hem of my thoughts, right there at the back.

I have forgotten to do something.

But what?

The night grows a little brighter as the moon slips out from behind a cloud. Her light makes the bronze of Rye's helmet shine bright as gold.

The helmet turns and the mouth smiles at me. Then I see the dark eyes go wide in the almond-shaped holes. Rye is looking at something behind me. I turn and I see the first of the enemy horsemen come over a hill to the south.

Help has come.

Not for us. For them.

Three hundred mounted men.

Lucky it is night.

Unlucky that Rye's helmet shines like a star in the moonlight.

I hear them raise the alarm.

14

THE HELMET

I sheathe my sword and bend to pick up two enemy javelins from the ground. With my left hand I grasp Rye's arm and tug. "Come on!" I cry. "They've seen us. Into the woods! To the city with seven hills! We've got to get our Leader or all is lost."

I pull him after me into the dark forest. It is a tangled wood, choked with scratching briars and black oaks. My lion skin is heavy and blocks my ears. All I can hear is my own panting. The thorns tug at the lion skin, but it protects me. The trail is narrow here, so I let go of Rye's hand. I'm not worried. He's a good runner, the best, and we know these woods.

Don't we?

The moon makes ink-black stripes in the trees and chinks of silver that look like the whites of eyes, so that it seems there are warriors or wild animals everywhere.

Behind me I hear a grunt. Rye has blundered into a tree and fallen back on the ground. I help him up. His face looks strange with the helmet covering it. I can only see his chin and mouth and eyes.

I see something in those eyes.

Something I have never seen before. Not even when he was six.

Fear.

"Don't worry, Rye!" I say. "Just follow me."

I should have told him to throw away that cursed helmet. Why didn't I?

15

CAPTURED

I can hear my heart pound as I run. My mouth is dry. The hot juice that flowed through my arms and legs has ebbed away.

The weight of my lion skin is too much, so I shrug it off.

I see a light ahead. Moonlight on grass. Then the black shape of an enemy rider. He is guarding the way out of the woods. He knows these parts better than I.

I swerve to try another route, almost invisible under a thick canopy of branches that blots out the moon. Without my lion skin, brambles prick my arms and briars scratch my legs. The sheltering forest has become hostile.

I try another way. But there is a guard there too.

And the next way.

The next, too!

At last I find a place where the enemy does not lie in wait. I burst out of the woods into the fresh air of safety. I see high fences and smell the comforting smell of grass, dung and cattle.

The moon is so bright that the grass seems white.

We are safe!

I turn to smile at Rye.

But he is not behind me.

"Oh, gods!" I cry.

Grief crashes over me and knocks me to my knees.

The moon is brilliant, harsh, angry.

"You abandoned your friend," she seems to say.

There is a sour taste in my mouth. The taste of fear.

I want to call out to Rye. But I'm afraid the men on horseback will hear me.

Instead, I dig my fingers into the ground and tear out clumps of earth. I lift my face to the sky and let out a silent howl.

Then I stand up and plunge back into the dark forest. I retrace my steps along invisible paths, all twisted and turning. It looks different on the way back. Everything looks different.

Then I hear a sound that whips my head around. Horses snorting, men shouting.

I fight my way to an opening in the leaves and peer out.

Rye stands in brilliant moonlight, surrounded by men on horseback. Our enemies!

Three of them are on the ground. Three more swing down from their horses.

Rye's head is bare. He has thrown away the helmet that betrayed him. He turns and tries to sprint for freedom.

But they clutch at him, catch him, hold him. They tear away his tunic, so his chest is bare, and he stands in only his leggings and boots.

In the eternity of that moment, I remember the foot race at the funeral games.

I was in the lead, with Salius just behind me and Rye in third.

But I slipped and fell. Without even thinking, I rolled in front of Salius and tripped him, too.

In this way, I helped Rye win first prize.

I would throw myself down again if it would help, but I know it won't.

What can I do?

I do the thing I should have done before we set out.

I do the thing that kept nagging at me.

I pray to Diana, goddess of the moon.

"Goddess of moon, stars and groves," I begin. "My father brought you offerings. My mother called on your name. I asked you to be my protector. Please help me now. Guide my aim."

I lift one of my javelins, balance it beside my ear and send it flying.

The goddess does not let me down.

My javelin flies true.

One of the men staggers, and turns. He looks down to see the bloody point of the javelin poking out of his tunic. Then a river of blood gushes from his chest. He falls, gasps, shudders.

His comrades look at him in horror. His eyes roll in his head and his lips burble blood.

My second javelin splits the air.

Then it splits the warm brain of a man who was foolish enough to remove his helmet.

Now I have no more javelins. I can only watch from the dark woods.

The biggest of the warriors bellows, "Who did this? I'll make you pay, whoever you are!"

He turns to Rye, held fast by two men. He raises his sword. Prepares to bury the blade in my friend's chest.

And now my feet are taking me out of the woods and into the clearing. My voice screams, "Me! Me! Kill me! The plan was mine. He is just a boy!"

But I am too late.

Time slows and I see the blade drive between Rye's ribs with such force that it shatters his breastbone. He sinks to his knees and sways. His lovely head droops like a poppy in the rain. He tries to lift it, but I see his life's blood gushing out, bathing his white chest and arms.

Once again, the red curtain falls over my eyes. My whole being screams my need for revenge. I charge towards the man who stabbed Rye.

But now I am surrounded, like a deer caught by hunting dogs. They prod me with their swords and bounce me from one to another like a feather ball. I barely feel their blows, their pokes, their slashes. I almost slip on my own blood, then I see the shouting face of the big man. The one who killed Rye. I raise my sword and cram it into his yelling mouth. I cut off his shout and his life, in one stab.

He is dying. But so am I.

With my last bit of strength, I crawl to my friend and cover his body with my own. I want to protect it from any further outrage.

"Rye," I whisper. "Little Rye. I'm sorry I couldn't save you, my friend."

With every fading drumbeat of my heart the world shrinks and shrinks and shrinks.

From high up I see our bodies lying there on the ground, and our black blood pooling on the moon-silver grass.

Then all is darkness.

– EURYALUS –

Hades. Hell. The Land of the Dead.

The sunny place where our Leader found his father and other heroes who had done brave deeds.

I am in none of those places.

I float above a marble city on the curve of a river. There is a temple on the highest of its seven hills. And pines like parasols.

And now I see a man in a courtyard below me. He is thin and bald, with a sad smile. He looks ordinary. But somehow I can see inside him. I see his spirit. It is the most beautiful thing I've ever seen. Like some kind of rock crystal filled with rainbows. It sparkles and glows. It is glorious.

Who is he? He paces up and down. He recites something in our language. In Latin.

It has the beat of poetry but I have never heard it before. He talks of Aeneas, our Leader!

He tells how the terrible warrior Turnus came at dawn and set fire to our fort. How many Trojans fell, but others fought back. How our Leader set off home and met water nymphs who told him to hurry.

The poet tells how, at last, our Leader won. He buried his sword in Turnus's heart. And married the princess. And founded a second Troy.

And now the man below stops writing and looks up. Not at me. But through me.

Then he speaks a name, and pairs it with another.

"Nisus," he says, "and Euryalus."

He bends over his tablet and writes, then reads what he has written in a low voice:

"You lucky two! If by chance my poem can give
Immortal life, your fame will always live.
Your souls will shine in many times and lands
And last as long as this Eternal City stands."

And all of a sudden, Nisus is beside me. He is as light as garlic skin. He hovers like a moth. But I can see he is smiling. He has found me. We have found each other.

"Who is he?" I look down at the man whose spirit brought us back together.

"He is Virgil," Nisus says. "And he has made us immortal with his words."

I put out my hand and feel him take it, a million years away.

"What is the Eternal City?" I ask.

"Rome," says Nisus. "The city of seven hills. It had a different name then, but it became a great city. You and I helped to found it," he adds.

"But we died," I say.

"Yes, but we helped a little."

"Will it last?" I ask.

"Forever," he says.

"And who am I?" I ask. I think I know but I need to be sure.

"You are Euryalus," he says. "We called you Rye. A Trojan. And my friend."

I look at him.

I remember.

"You died for me," I say. "That is True Glory. That is why he is telling our story. That is why we still live."

He shrugs, smiles, nods.

Already he seems less moth-like. More solid. More Nisus.

I might forget my name but I will never forget his.

Long ago I said, "I don't care where I go after death, as long as we're together."

Now we will be together. We will live together for all time.

Thanks to the poet Virgil, who made us immortal.